BBC CHILDREN'S BOOKS
Published by the Penguin Group
Penguin Books Ltd, 80 Strand, London WC2R 0RL, England
Penguin Books Australia Ltd, 250 Camberwell Road,
Camberwell, Victoria 3124, Australia
First published by BBC Worldwide Ltd, 1999
Text and design © BBC Children's Books, 1999
This edition published by BBC Children's Books, 2005
CBeebies & logo™ BBC. © BBC 2002
10 9 8 7 6 5 4 3 2 1
Written by Diane Redmond
Based upon the television series
Bob the Builder © 2005 HIT Entertainment PLC and Keith Chapman.
The Bob the Builder name and character and the Wendy, Spud, Roley,
Muck, Pilchard, Dizzy, Lofty and Scoop characters are trademarks of
HIT Entertainment PLC. Registered in the UK.
With thanks to HOT Animation
www.bobthebuilder.com
ISBN 1 405 90072 5
Printed in Italy

Bob's Bugle

Bob was busy mending a broken central heating system. Muck was helping him.

"Now that the hot water tank is fitted, it's time to check the pipes!" Bob explained to Muck.

One of the pipes was blocked by a little bit of dirt. Bob blew down the pipe and the dirt popped out.

Bleurgh-boo-boo-bloooh! whistled the pipe, as Bob blew through it.

"Listen to this, Muck!" laughed Bob, and he blew again.

T-o-o-o -t-tee-toooooot-tooooooot!

"What is it... a frog with a sore throat?" Muck asked.

"No!" said Bob, excitedly. "It's my bugle! Or it will be, when I've finished making it!"

"What's a bugle?" Muck asked.

"It's a musical instrument," Bob explained. "You blow in one end and a loud noise comes out of the other end."

Back at the yard, Wendy was staring into space, looking thoughtful.

"What are you thinking about?" asked Scoop.

"Some friends of mine have moved to a new house and I want to buy them a gift, but I can't think what to get!" answered Wendy.

Just then Muck and Bob roared into the yard. Bob hurried into his workshop and shut the door.

The machines and Wendy clustered outside.
They could hear strange bangs and clanks.
Suddenly, a loud parp! made them jump.
Bob came out of his workshop, waving his
shiny new bugle.

"What's that awful noise?" cried Wendy.

"Shhh Wendy," whispered Muck. "It's Bob's new bugle, and he thinks it's great!"

"So do I!" rumbled Roley.

"Perhaps I could join a band!" chuckled Bob.

"You'll have to practise if you want to be in a band," said Roley.

"You're right," agreed Bob.

"Can I practise? Yes I can!"

Bob practised his bugle all night long.

Bloo-hoo-doo-diddley-diddley-doo!

"I want to go to sleep!" wailed Scoop.

"Shall we, er... tell Bob we don't like it...?" Lofty wondered.

"Hey, come on!" rumbled Roley. "Bob's having fun!"

The tired machines listened as the bugle blasts slowly turned to weak toot-toots then one last paaarp.

"Thank goodness he's stopped!" gasped Scoop.

The next morning, Wendy was still trying to think of a special present for her friends.

"I hardly slept last night, worrying about it," she said.

"We hardly slept last night because of Bob playing his bugle!" grumbled Muck.

Just then, Bob came into the yard, playing his bugle.

"Come on, Muck!" Bob called. "We've got work to do." And as he walked into his workshop, he carefully put his bugle by the door.

"Now's our chance, Lofty! Grab the bugle!" said Scoop.

Lofty extended his crane and hooked the bugle onto it.

"Put it on the roof. Bob will never find it there!" said Dizzy.

Carefully, Lofty put the bugle on the roof.

But then Bird hopped over to the bugle and started to push it with his beak.

"Oh no!" cried Muck as the bugle rolled off the roof into his scoop.

"What was that?" called Bob.

"Nothing!" said Muck.

"Come on, Muck. We've got to finish that central heating job!" said Bob.

While Bob packed his tools, Muck looked for somewhere to hide the bugle. Dizzy ran up to him and tipped her mixer forwards.

"Stick it in here," she whispered.

But then disaster struck!

"I'll need you too, Dizzy!" called Bob.

"Me! Why?" she said nervously.

"To mix concrete, of course!" replied Bob.

At the house, Bob went inside to fix the radiators.

"Ding-a-dong-a-ding!" he sang, as he tapped the radiators with his hammer.

"Nice music, but not as good as my bugle!" Bob said.

Outside, Dizzy and Muck wondered what to do with the bugle.

Suddenly, Bob appeared at the door with a bucket.

"Cement please Dizzy!" he said

"Are you sure?" gulped Dizzy.

"Of course I'm sure!" laughed Bob.

"Here goes..." sighed Dizzy. She poured the cement into Bob's bucket.

Glug-glug-glug-CLANG! Bob's bugle, covered in cement, fell into the bucket.

"How did that get there?" Bob cried with disbelief.

"No idea!" mumbled Muck and Dizzy.

"Never mind – I'll soon have it cleaned up," smiled Bob.

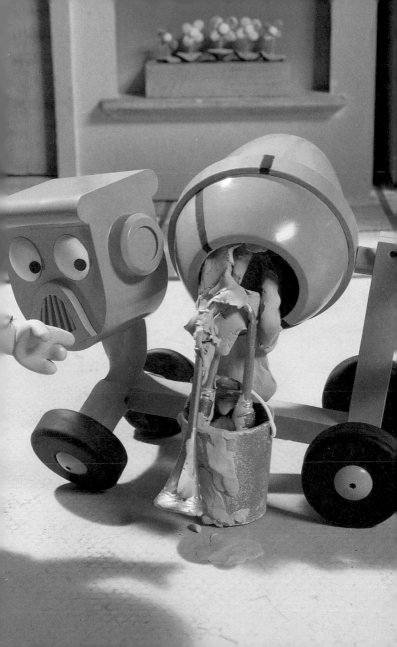

Back at the yard, Bob cleaned his dirty bugle carefully. Then he gently put it on the ground.

"Roley, can you help me over here for a minute?" called Bob.

"Ok, Bob," rumbled Roley.

As he rolled forwards there was a terrible crunch! Roley had squashed Bob's bugle!

"Oh, no! I'm so sorry Bob!" cried Roley.

Bob could see that Roley was upset.

"Don't worry. I shouldn't have left it on the ground," sighed Bob. As he picked up the flattened bugle, the broken pieces went tinkle, tinkle.

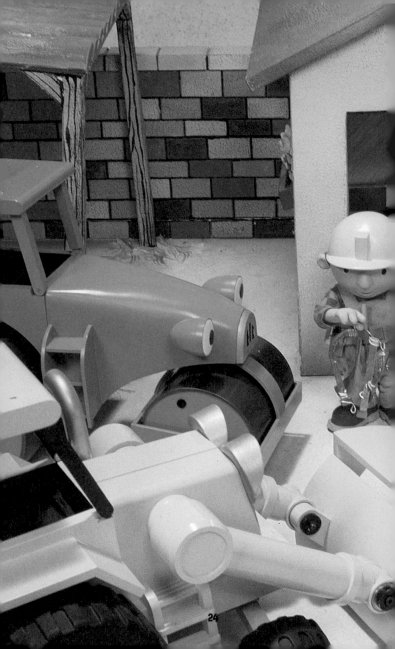

"That's a lovely set of wind chimes," said Wendy, coming out of her office. "Just the sort of present I've been looking for!"

"There I was, thinking I'd made a bugle, when it was really a set of wind chimes!" smiled Bob. "You can have these for your friends, Wendy."

"Thanks, Bob," cried Wendy, shaking the chimes.

Tinkle, tinkle, tinkle!

"Ah..." sighed Scoop. "Nice, quiet wind chimes..."

"I quite liked the bugle myself!" rumbled Roley.

THE END!